Snoopy and Friends

🅖 A GOLDEN BOOK • NEW YORK

Copyright © 2015 by Peanuts Worldwide LLC
Copyright © 2015 Twentieth Century Fox Film Corporation
All rights reserved.
Published in the United States by Golden Books, an imprint of Random House Children's Books,
a division of Penguin Random House LLC, 1745 Broadway, New York, NY 10019, and in Canada
by Random House of Canada, a division of Penguin Random House Ltd., Toronto. Originally published
by Western Publishing Company, Inc., in 1988. Golden Books, A Golden Book, A Little Golden Book,
the G colophon, and the distinctive gold spine are registered trademarks
of Penguin Random House LLC.
randomhousekids.com
Educators and librarians, for a variety of teaching tools, visit us at RHTeachersLibrarians.com
ISBN 978-1-101-93515-6 (trade) — ISBN 978-1-101-93516-3 (ebook)
Printed in the United States of America
10 9 8 7 6 5 4 3 2 1

D1301055

Good ol' Charlie Brown almost never wins. But he never gives up.

Charlie Brown's best friend is his
dog, the world-famous beagle, Snoopy.

Charlie Brown always looks
forward to baseball season. He is
the manager and pitcher . . . and
his team has never won a game.

Charlie Brown can never get a kite in the air, but he never stops trying.

Snoopy's sidekick is a little yellow bird named Woodstock.

Chirping in a language only Snoopy
understands, Woodstock is never far
from Snoopy's doghouse.

As the Flying Ace, Snoopy chases
the notorious Red Baron, rescuing the
beautiful Fifi.

Spike, Olaf, and
Belle are just a few of
Snoopy's brothers and
sisters. They were all
puppies together on
the farm.

Charlie Brown's friend Linus is the philosopher of the gang. He loves his blue blanket, which makes a great slingshot.

Charlie Brown's little sister, Sally,
loves Linus. Sally has a lot of questions—
especially "Why won't my Sweet Babboo
pay attention to me?"

Linus's big sister, Lucy, is bossy and crabby. She is also ambitious—one day she wants to be president and queen.

Lucy's only weakness is the musical
genius Schroeder.

She really likes him, but Schroeder only
has eyes for Beethoven.

Lucy loves to play tricks on Charlie
Brown. No matter how many times she
promises to hold the football for him, she
always pulls it away right before he kicks it.

But Lucy is always willing to lend an ear
and listen to Charlie Brown's troubles—
for a nickel, of course.

Franklin, Marcie, and Peppermint Patty go to school with the rest of the gang. Franklin is kind and loves hockey.

Peppermint Patty is a natural athlete, and Marcie is a good student. They both are good friends with Charlie Brown.

Charlie Brown wants to be friends
with the little red-haired girl at school.

He is too shy to talk to her, so
he doesn't even know her name.

Frieda loves her naturally curly hair.
Violet thinks Snoopy is very cute.

Pig-Pen travels with his own private
dust storm, but his friend Charlie Brown
doesn't mind.

After school,
Charlie Brown and
his friends love
to have fun together.
In wintertime, they
skate on the pond.

Isn't it nice to have friends?